O9-BUD-738

Library of Congress Cataloging in Publication Data:
Roberts, Sarah. Ernie's big mess. (Sesame Street start-to-read books) SUMMARY: Bert and Ernie
argue over Ernie's messiness, so Ernie looks for another place to stay. [1. Cleanliness—Fiction]
I. Henson, Jim. II. Mathieu, Joseph. III. Children's Television Workshop. IV. Sesame Street.
V. Title. VI. Series. PZ7.R54428Er [Fic] AACR2 81-2464 ISBN: 0-394-84847-0 (trade);
0-394-94847-5 (lib. bdg.) Manufactured in the United States of America

21 22 23 24 25 26 27 28 29 30

A Sesame Street Start-to-Read Book™

Ernie's Big Mess

by Sarah Roberts • illustrated by Joe Mathieu

Featuring Jim Henson's Sesame Street Muppets

Random House/Children's Television Workshop

Bert and Ernie are best friends.
They live together.
Bert is neat.
Ernie is messy.

Sometimes Ernie is VERY messy.

Then Bert gets mad.

"Ernie, come here!" Bert shouts.

"Look at the mess you have made!"

"Okay, Bert," says Ernie.
"I am coming."

Ernie jumps out of the tub.

Splash! Splash!

Ernie splashes water on the floor.

Drip. Drip.

He drips water on the rug.

"Ernie!" Bert shouts.
"You are making
a BIGGER mess!"
Ernie smiles at Bert.
"But, Bert," Ernie says,
"you told me to look
at the mess I made."

Now Bert is very angry.
"I wish I lived here
all by myself!" he shouts.
Bert walks out of the room.
SLAM! goes the door.

Ernie stops smiling.

"Bert does not want me here
anymore," he says.

"I guess I will go away."

Ernie is sad.

Ernie gets dressed.

Then he packs a big bag.

"Come on, Rubber Duckie,"

Ernie says.

"We have to go."

Ernie closes the door softly.
"Good-bye, house," he says.
"I will miss you."

Ernie drags his bag
down Sesame Street.
He goes to see Big Bird.
"Ernie, it is late!"
says Big Bird.
"You should be in bed."

"I have no bed," says Ernie.
"Bert is mad at me.
I have to find
a new home."

"You can stay with me,"
says Big Bird.
"My nest is a nice place
to sleep."

Ernie climbs into the nest.
"Ouch!" says Ernie.
"This is NOT
    a nice place to sleep.
It is full of sticks!"

Ernie climbs out of the nest.
"Good night, Big Bird," he says.
Then he goes to Grover's house.

"Ernie, it is late!
   You should be in bed,"
   says Grover.
"I have no bed," says Ernie.
"Bert is mad at me.
   I have to find
   a new home."

"You can share my little bed,"
says Grover.
Ernie climbs into Grover's bed.
"Do you like my soft little bed?"
Grover asks.
"Well, it is soft," says Ernie.

Then Ernie turns over.
CRASH! He falls onto the floor.
"Grover, this bed is TOO little!"

Ernie leaves Grover's house
with his big bag.
He is very tired.
Then he sees Oscar's
trash can.

BANG! BANG!
Ernie bangs on
the trash can.
"Oscar, are you sleeping?"
Ernie asks.

"I was sleeping," says Oscar.
"Now I am awake."
Oscar the Grouch is mad.
"Oscar, where can I find
a big soft bed?" Ernie asks.

"A big soft bed?" yells Oscar.
"Soft beds are yucchy!"
BANG! goes the lid
of the trash can.

"Oh dear," says Ernie.
"Where can I sleep?
I am so tired."
Ernie sits down.
Soon he is asleep.

Sesame Street is quiet.

Everyone is sleeping.

Everyone but Bert.

Bert is looking for Ernie.

He wakes up Big Bird.

"Big Bird, have you
seen Ernie?" asks Bert.

"He was here," says Big Bird.

"But he is not here anymore."

Then Bert goes to Grover's house.
"Grover, have you
  seen Ernie?" asks Bert.
"He was here," says Grover.
"But he is not here anymore."

Bert walks down the street.

He is very sad.

"Ernieee!" he calls.

"Where are you?"

Then he sees Ernie.

"Ernie, are you okay?" asks Bert.
"Sure, Bert. I was just sleeping,"
   says Ernie.

Bert picks up Ernie's bag.
"Come on home, old pal,"
he says. "I am sorry
I yelled at you."

Bert and Ernie go home.
"Gee, Bert," says Ernie,
"it is good to be home."
He opens his big bag.
All his toys fall out.

"I am sorry, Bert.
I made a mess again,"
says Ernie.
"That is okay," says Bert.
"We will clean it up
in the morning."

Ernie and Bert are ready for bed.

"I am glad you are home," says Bert.

"Me too," says Ernie.

"Good night, Bert."

"Good night, Ernie."